Published by Scholastic Inc.
90 Old Sherman Turnpike, Danbury, Connecticut 06816.

For information regarding permission, write to:
Disney Licensed Publishing
114 Fifth Avenue, New York, New York 10011.

ISBN 0-7172-6808-X

Designed and produced by Bill SMITH STUDIO.

Printed in the U.S.A.
First printing, November 2003

The Big Race

A Story About *Loyalty*

by **S.R. Baecker**
illustrated by
S.I. International

SCHOLASTIC INC.

New York   Toronto   London   Auckland   Sydney
Mexico City   New Delhi   Hong Kong   Buenos Aires

$\mathcal{P}$ocahontas and Nakoma peered over the edge of the cliff.

"Oh, this is high," Nakoma said, hesitantly.

"Yes, it is," replied Pocahontas. "But we need to run, swim, canoe, *and* dive in tomorrow's race. You can do it."

"*I* hope you're right," Nakoma said. Then she stepped to the edge and took a deep breath. "E-e-e-o-o-o-o!" she screamed, pushing off from the edge.

*K*ocoum and his friend Lucalla were fishing nearby and heard Nakoma's scream echo through the woods.

"*D*id you hear that?" Kocoum asked. "Someone must be hurt!"

"No," said Lucalla, laughing. "That's Pocahontas and Nakoma. They're practicing for the Harvest Festival Race. Let's go and watch."

*K*ocoum and Lucalla reached the base of the cliff just as Pocahontas pushed off into the air. Spreading her arms wide, she looked like a graceful bird gliding through the air.

$\mathcal{T}$hen Pocahontas brought her arms together over her head and hit the water with a tiny splash.

"That was perfect!" Nakoma yelled when Pocahontas popped up to the surface.

"Hello, Pocahontas," Lucalla yelled from shore. "Nakoma's right, that was a beautiful dive." "Thank you, Lucalla," Pocahontas replied. Then she and Nakoma swam to shore.

"*A*re you preparing for the big race tomorrow?" Kocoum asked.

"Yes, we are," said Nakoma. "Pocahontas has been helping me practice all day."

"You're lucky to have such a loyal friend," Lucalla responded.

"You don't expect to win, do you?" asked Kocoum.

"Yes, Kocoum, we do," replied Pocahontas.

"𝒩o one dives more gracefully than you, Pocahontas," Kocoum said. "And Nakoma, you run like the swiftest deer. But for canoe racing, you need the strength of a tribal warrior."

"The river is running strong," Kocoum
warned. "It will carry you to the great water.
And then some other braves and I will have to
rescue you."

"*W*e will not need you or any other braves to rescue us, Kocoum," Pocahontas said proudly. "Let's go, Nakoma. We'll paddle the river once more before going home for dinner."

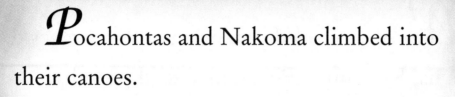

Pocahontas and Nakoma climbed into their canoes.

"Are you sure you don't mind helping me?" Nakoma asked. "After all, we will be competing against each other tomorrow."

"Nakoma, our friendship is much more important than any contest," Pocahontas said. "We'll just do the best we can."

"*B*esides," Pocahontas said, laughing, "I just want to beat Kocoum in the canoe race!"

"I'll be happy if I can just finish it," Nakoma said. "That cliff is so high, and Kocoum was right—the river is running strong! I hope I can do it."

"We'll do it together," Pocahontas said. "You'll see."

Then pulling ahead of Nakoma, Pocahontas shouted, "Come on, we'll race back to the cliff!"

$\mathcal{F}$inally, the big day arrived. Everyone was excited and ready to enjoy the village's annual Harvest Festival.

"The Harvest Festival Race is about to begin!" Chief Powhatan announced in his big, booming voice.

$\mathcal{E}$veryone became quiet while the chief described the course to the racers.

"Contestants, race to the cliff, dive into the river, and swim to shore. Then you will get your canoe, paddle upstream to where the river forks, and return to finish at the base of the cliff."

$\mathcal{T}$he chief raised his arms high above his head.

"Begin the race!" he bellowed.

The racers darted off down the path.

Nakoma quickly took the lead. Her feet were barely touching the ground as she seemed to fly down the path.

*N*akoma hesitated at the edge of the cliff, while two other racers dived into the water.

"You can do it, you can do it," she repeated to herself. Then she pushed off with her legs and dived into the river.

Nakoma was near the shore by the time Pocahontas reached the cliff. She looked over the edge quickly to make sure no one was below her and then flew into the air.

*K*ocoum dived right after Pocahontas and entered the water with a huge splash.

They reached the shore at almost the same time and ran to their canoes.

*P*ocahontas and Kocoum passed one canoe, then another.

"Go, Pocahontas, go!" Nakoma yelled when they zoomed past her.

"You're doing really well, Nakoma!" Pocahontas shouted back.

"Wait for me at the finish line!" Nakoma yelled.

*T*hen suddenly Pocahontas heard a loud scream from behind her.

"Whoooooaaaaaaa!"

Splash!

It was Nakoma! She had been thrown into the river when her canoe hit some underwater rocks.

$\mathcal{N}$akoma was okay, but her paddle and canoe were quickly floating away from her.

"Hey, Nakoma—you're going the wrong way!" one of the braves shouted when he passed Nakoma swimming after her canoe.

"It's a canoe *race*—not a canoe chase!" shouted Lucalla.

"Are you okay?" Pocahontas yelled.

"I'm fine," Nakoma yelled back. "Wet, but fine.
Don't worry about me. Finish the race!"

What would a princess do?

Pocahontas quickly turned around. "Get your canoe—I'll get the paddle!" Pocahontas yelled, racing past Nakoma.

Minutes later, Pocahontas plucked the paddle out of the river and headed back upstream.

Meanwhile, Nakoma finally reached her canoe.

"*I*'m sorry I made you lose the race," Nakoma muttered, pulling herself into her canoe.

"Oh, Nakoma, you didn't *make* me lose," Pocahontas said. "Helping you is more important than winning a race."

Nakoma smiled and said, "You are a loyal friend. Lucalla was right, I am lucky."

"*A*nyway," Pocahontas said in a deep voice like Kocoum's, "I couldn't let the river carry you to the great water where Kocoum and the big, strong, brave warriors would have to rescue you."

Nakoma laughed so hard at Pocahontas's imitation of Kocoum that she almost tipped over her canoe again.

*R*ealizing how far behind they now were, Nakoma groaned. "Oh, we'll never catch up now."

"Maybe not," said Pocahontas. "But this race isn't over until you and I finish it—together."

As Pocahontas and Nakoma paddled to shore, the chief and Kocoum walked up to them.

"You showed great loyalty to Nakoma today, Daughter," the chief said. "I'm very proud of you."

"Thank you, Pocahontas," Nakoma said, as she hugged her best friend.

The End